THE CREEPY CLASSICS

CHILDREN'S COLLECTION

Dados Internacionais de Catalogação na Publicação (CIP) de acordo com ISBD

S847m   Stevenson, Robert Louis.
           Dr. Jekyll and Mr. Hyde / Robert Louis Stevenson. - Jandira, SP : W. Books, 2025.
           120 p. ; 12,80cm x 19,80cm. - (Classics).

           ISBN: 978-65-5294-190-9

           1. Literatura inglesa. 2. Terror. 3. Clássicos. 4. Fantasia. 5. Imaginação. 6. Suspense.
           I. Título. II. Série.

2025-2534   CDD 823.91
                                                                                                           CDU 821.111-3

Elaborada por Lucio Feitosa - CRB-8/8803
Índice para catálogo sistemático:
1. Literatura inglesa 823.91
2. Literatura inglesa 821.111-3

The Creepy Classics Collection
Text © Sweet Cherry Publishing Limited, 2024
Inside illustrations © Sweet Cherry Publishing Limited, 2024
Cover illustrations © Sweet Cherry Publishing Limited, 2024

Text based on the original story by Robert Louis Stevenson,
adapted by Gemma Barder
Illustrations by Nick Moffatt

© 2025 edition:
Ciranda Cultural Editora e Distribuidora Ltda.

1st edition in 2025
www.cirandacultural.com.br
No part of this publication may be reproduced, stored in a retrieval system, or transmitted in any form or by any means, electronic, mechanical, photocopying, recording, or otherwise, without written permission of the publisher.
This book is a work of fiction. Names, characters, places, and incidents are either the product of the author's imagination or are used fictitiously, and any resemblance to actual persons, living or dead, business establishments, events, or locales is entirely coincidental.

Dr Jekyll
and Mr Hyde

Robert Louis Stevenson

GABRIEL UTTERSON
A lawyer

RICHARD ENFIELD
Gabriel's cousin

MR GUEST
Gabriel's secretary

DR LANYON
A friend of Gabriel and
Dr Jekyll

Chapter One

Each Sunday afternoon, Gabriel Utterson met his cousin Richard Enfield at Regent's Park in London. Although the two men had very little in common, they both enjoyed the other's company and spent their walks catching up with each other's news.

'Something very strange happened to me on this very street the other evening,' said Richard, when they had left the park and begun the journey home through the busy streets of London. 'I was walking home from the theatre when I saw a man run past and knock over a little girl!'

'How awful!' replied Gabriel.

'What did you do?'

'I managed to catch the man before he ran off,' Richard continued. 'A crowd of onlookers gathered to see if the little girl was all right, but it was clear she would need to see a doctor.'

'Poor little thing,' replied Gabriel. 'And doctors can be expensive. What happened to the man?'

'He was forced to give the girl some money to pay for the doctor,' said Richard. 'He disappeared inside that door right there.' He pointed his cane at the second door down from the corner on the left. It was an ancient, battered thing, with no bell or knocker, set in a two-storey building with no windows. It was clearly not a shop

like most of the other buildings. Nor did it look like a house.

'Then,' Richard continued, 'the man reappeared a moment later with a cheque for almost £100. It was signed by a Dr Jekyll, I think his name was.'

Gabriel stopped walking. 'Dr Jekyll?' he said. 'I know him! He is a friend and one of my clients, not to mention a well-respected scientist. He lives close to here. I would not have thought he could do something so horrible!'

cheque
A signed piece of paper that is exchanged at a bank for money.

'No, no,' said Richard, quickly reassuring his cousin. 'Dr Jekyll wrote the cheque, but the man who knocked over the little girl was called Mr Hyde.'

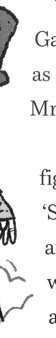

They walked on. Gabriel said nothing as Richard described Mr Hyde.

'He was a strange figure,' said Richard. 'Smaller than you and I. He walked with a hunch and kept his face turned away as he spoke. I took a huge dislike to his appearance and his character – as did the other people here at the time. He did not seem sorry for what he'd done, only keen to get away from us all. I have never seen an angrier crowd. They looked as if they wanted to tear him limb from limb!'

Again, Gabriel said nothing on the subject of Mr Hyde, although he listened with interest. Eventually, the cousins' conversation drifted away from Richard's story, and they finished their walk, promising to meet again the following Sunday. Once he had returned home, Gabriel went straight to his study and looked through his files. As a lawyer, Gabriel helped people to sort out all kinds of complicated things. Things such as buying a house or writing a will so that everyone knew what to do with your possessions when you died. He had even helped to write his friend Dr Jekyll's will. This was the document he looked at now.

'I knew I recognised that name,' he said.

Dr Jekyll's will stated that if Dr Jekyll died or simply disappeared for longer than three months without explanation, he wanted all his money and his home to go to a man called Mr Hyde.

The same man from Richard's story.

Chapter Two

Gabriel and Dr Jekyll shared a friend whose name was Dr Lanyon, and whose home they had often dined at together in the past. Despite being around the same age as Dr Jekyll and Gabriel, Dr Lanyon had the white hair and good sense of someone older.
He had known Gabriel at school

and at college, and they were Dr Jekyll's oldest friends. Both had known Dr Jekyll before he was the well-respected scientist he was now; back when he was a wild young man often in trouble.

For that reason, it was Dr Lanyon who Gabriel first thought of after hearing Richard's story and re-reading Dr Jekyll's will. He was sure that Dr Lanyon would know if their friend was mixing with the wrong sort of people. So the next morning, Gabriel went to visit him.

'This Mr Hyde is a bad person, I am sure,' said Gabriel, after he had explained everything to Dr Lanyon. 'To hurt a little girl, try to run away and then get Jekyll to pay for the little girl's doctor seems very strange. What do you think it means?'

Dr Lanyon sighed as he passed Gabriel a cup of tea. 'I agree with you,' he said. 'It does seem very strange indeed, but I am afraid I don't think I can help you. Jekyll and I have not seen or spoken to each other for a long time.'

Gabriel looked at Dr Lanyon with surprise. 'Why ever not?' he asked.

Dr Lanyon looked uncomfortable and shifted in his seat.

'Well, you see … I did not approve of some of Jekyll's experiments.'

'Experiments?' Gabriel repeated.

'Yes,' replied Dr Lanyon. 'Jekyll is an excellent scientist, but some years back he began to have some very *un*scientific ideas. As I am a medical doctor, I don't think about science in the same way that he does. He did not like my opinion on his work, so I am sorry to say we fell out.'

Gabriel was concerned to hear this. Dr Lanyon was such a friendly, agreeable man that he could not see how anyone could ever fall out with him. If Dr Jekyll was losing friends like Dr Lanyon and picking up friends like Mr Hyde, he must surely be in some sort of trouble.

Gabriel wanted to ask Dr Lanyon more about Dr Jekyll's strange experiments, but he could tell that his old friend did not want to say any more on the matter. And so they talked of other things until the visit was over.

Chapter Three

In the days after Gabriel's visit to Dr Lanyon's house, he often

walked by the spot where his cousin, Richard, had first spotted Mr Hyde. He did this deliberately, hoping to see the man himself.

He was not successful, but this only made him more determined: *If he is Mr Hyde,* he thought to himself, *then I shall be Mr Seek.*

Eventually, Gabriel's efforts paid off. One day, he passed down the busy shopping street and saw a hunched figure in a hat outside the door from Richard's story. As Gabriel watched, the man put a key into his pocket.

'Excuse me!' called Gabriel,

moving quickly towards him, but the figure moved more quickly still. By the time Gabriel reached the end of the street, the figure had disappeared.

Gabriel suddenly felt cold. Something about the sighting troubled him, and Gabriel was almost glad that whoever it was had not stopped when he called out. Could it have been the mysterious Mr Hyde?

He turned the corner from the shopping street to a handsome square of buildings one street over. Once grand houses, many of them had been split into flats, as well as offices for mapmakers, architects, lawyers – and doctors.

In all this time Gabriel had not asked Dr Jekyll directly about Mr Hyde, but he now decided to do just that. He approached the nicest of the buildings, two down from the corner on the left, and knocked. The door was answered by a well-dressed, elderly butler.

'Good day, Poole,' Gabriel greeted the man. 'Is Dr Jekyll at home?'

Poole replied that his master was away. The butler looked pale and his eyes shifted as he spoke. Gabriel had met Poole many times over the years and this behaviour was not normal for him.

'Is everything all right, Poole?' asked Gabriel.

'To be honest, Mr Utterson, no,' Poole replied, quietly. He was a good butler and did not want to look like he was telling tales on his master. 'The other servants and I are terribly worried about the doctor.' He stood aside to let Gabriel into the well-decorated hallway and shut the door behind him.

'Dr Jekyll has become friends with a very strange fellow,' continued Poole. 'His name is Mr Hyde. He started coming to the house a few months ago, although no one ever lets him

in through the front door. We think the doctor may have given him a key to his laboratory.'

'The laboratory?' Gabriel repeated. 'Where is that?' He had visited Dr Jekyll's house many times and never seen such a room, though he realised now that it made sense for there to be one. Dr Jekyll was a scientist, after all.

'Oh, it is not part of the main

---

laboratory
A place used for scientific investigation and experiments.

house, sir,' Poole explained. 'You have to go through the courtyard at the back. The laboratory is in a separate block that opens out onto the street behind us. Mr Hyde comes and goes through it as he pleases.'

So the strange building that is neither a shop nor a house is Dr Jekyll's laboratory, Gabriel realised. But all he said was, 'Dr Jekyll must have a lot of trust in Mr Hyde to give him a key to his home.'

'Yes, sir, but …'

'But what?'

'Mr Hyde is horrible, sir!' said Poole. 'He shouts and stomps about the place. He always wears a dark cloak, and I have even seen him in the doctor's own clothes – although they are far too big for him. We think he might be blackmailing the doctor with some secret from his past.'

Gabriel was shocked to hear what Poole was telling him, but it was starting to make sense.

blackmail
The use of threats to force someone to pay money or do something.

Dr Jekyll had been known to get into trouble in his younger years, a very long time ago. If this Mr Hyde held some dark secret over Dr Jekyll's head, he could have forced him to change his will. Mr Hyde would inherit all of Dr Jekyll's money and his townhouse if Dr Jekyll died. And Mr Hyde could very well be the one to kill him if his attitude towards the poor girl in Richard's story was anything to go by.

'Thank you for telling me all this, Poole,' said Gabriel at last. 'I shall try to keep an eye on the doctor – and on this Mr Hyde, too.'

CHAPTER FOUR

A week later, Gabriel was at home working at his desk when there was a loud knock on the front door. A moment later, Gabriel's secretary, Mr Guest, showed a tall man into Gabriel's study.

'Sorry to disturb you, sir,' said Mr Guest. 'There is an Inspector Newcomen to see you from Scotland Yard.'

'Good morning, Inspector Newcomen,' said Gabriel, a look of

concern on his face as he stood up. 'What can I help you with?'

The police inspector pulled a piece of paper from his pocket. With a shock, Gabriel noticed that it was stained with blood.

'I believe you know a Sir Danvers Carew,' the inspector said.

Gabriel nodded. 'Why, yes, he is a client of mine – a very nice old fellow, too.'

'I'm sorry to inform you that Sir Danvers Carew was killed last night.' The inspector handed the bloodstained paper to Gabriel. 'This was found in his coat pocket.'

Gabriel took the piece of paper with a trembling hand. It was a letter from Gabriel's own office confirming an appointment that he and Sir Danvers Carew were meant to have the following week.

Gabriel's knees felt a little weak and he sat heavily on his desk chair. 'How dreadful …'

'There is a witness who says the man who committed the crime was called Hyde,' the inspector said. Gabriel's eyes shot up. 'As you knew the old gentleman who has been killed,' added the inspector, 'we wondered if you might know why this Mr Hyde would have killed him.'

Gabriel searched his mind for a connection. He was shocked and saddened to hear of Sir Danvers Carew's death. He had been a kind old man with lots of friends and family. Why *anyone* would want to kill him was beyond understanding, and why the mysterious Mr Hyde would want to was even more so.

'I'm afraid I can't tell you why Mr Hyde would do such a thing,' said Gabriel. 'I have never met the man, but I can give you his address.'

Gabriel stood up and opened a tall cabinet containing all the paperwork for his clients. He picked out Dr Jekyll's file and scanned the documents for Mr Hyde's details. Dr Jekyll had given him Mr Hyde's address when he made his will. But at the last moment, Gabriel thought better of simply handing the information over. He was still too curious about Mr Hyde, and once the police had him, he would have no chance to see the strange man for himself. He had to go there with the inspector.

'As a matter of fact,' Gabriel said, 'I can take you to him this very minute.'

At the police inspector's nod, Gabriel pocketed the address and threw on his coat and hat. He hailed a carriage for himself and the inspector. Before long they had driven to a gloomy, run-down part of town, where a tall wooden building divided into small flats stood.

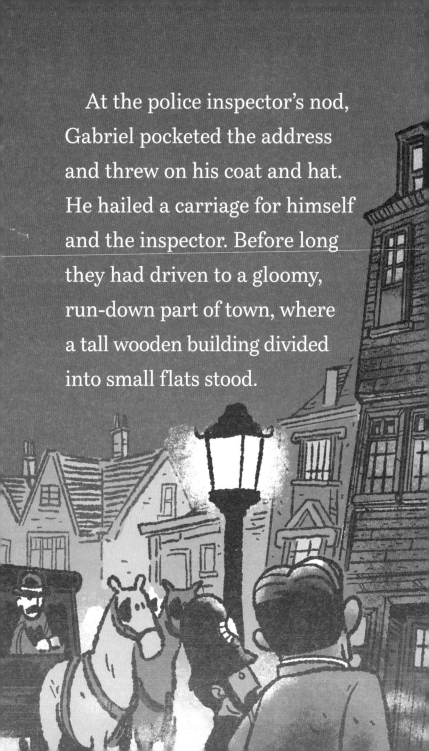

When there was no answer at Mr Hyde's door, the police inspector asked the landlady to open it for them.

'There you go,' said the silver-haired woman, swinging open the door. 'Although you won't find much – 'e's 'ardly ever 'ere.'

'What do you mean?' asked Gabriel as the police inspector looked around the flat, which was much nicer inside than it was outside. Gabriel was surprised by the good taste shown in the choice of furniture and paintings. He watched as Inspector Newcomen carefully opened cupboards and prodded the remains of burnt papers in the cold fireplace. He was looking for evidence for the murder case.

'I mean that Mr 'yde comes and goes, but 'e never stays for long,' said the landlady. 'Don't know why Dr Jekyll keeps paying the rent for 'im to be honest with you.'

Gabriel's blood ran cold. Dr Jekyll was paying for Mr Hyde's flat. He had also given the man a key to his own house and was apparently lending him his own clothes. Add to that the fact that

Mr Hyde had been included in Dr Jekyll's will and was now suspected of murder.

Gabriel was more concerned than ever for the well-being of his friend.

Chapter Five

When he had finished searching Mr Hyde's flat, Inspector Newcomen had found the burnt stub of a green chequebook and what looked like a broken cane. This last item interested him greatly.

'This appears to be part of the murder weapon,' he explained.

He thanked Gabriel

for his help and promised to keep him informed as the case progressed.

Gabriel was exhausted, but he decided to visit Dr Jekyll once again to try to make some sense of the situation.

'I am glad to see you, sir,' said Poole, opening the door and welcoming Gabriel inside Dr Jekyll's house. 'Dr Jekyll is in his library, but I'm afraid that he is not feeling his best today.'

'I am sorry to hear that,' replied Gabriel, handing his coat and hat to Poole.

'I am sure seeing a friend will do him some good,' said Poole, leading Gabriel to the library.

Dr Jekyll was sitting by the fire with a blanket over his knees. He was a large man with a certain craftiness to his face. His chin, usually smooth-shaven, was today

shadowed with stubble. The rest of his face was pale and gaunt, his eyes haunted and circled with dark rings. He managed a sickly smile when he saw his friend.

'Utterson, what a pleasure to see you,' Dr Jekyll said, gesturing to the seat opposite him without standing.

'How are you?' said Gabriel, sitting down. 'Poole said you were not well?'

The smile died on Dr Jekyll's lips. 'It is true. I have not been feeling like myself recently,' he said. 'Not at all. But enough of that – what brings you here today?'

'I wanted to ask you about this Mr Hyde fellow you have befriended,' said Gabriel. 'I fear he is in some trouble and that you may be dragged into it with him.'

Dr Jekyll looked away. 'It is true,' he said in a quiet voice.

'Mr Hyde *was* a friend of sorts, for a short time, but he is gone now.'

'Thank goodness!' cried Gabriel, relief overwhelming him. 'Do you know he has been accused of killing Sir Danvers Carew?'

Dr Jekyll covered his face with his hands. 'I do,' he said, tears falling down his cheeks. 'I know, although I wish I did not. And I wish I could tell you where Mr Hyde is now, but I can't. All I know is that he has gone away, and I pray it is for good. He gave me that letter this morning before he went.'

Shocked by his friend's tears, Gabriel picked up a letter that was sitting on Dr Jekyll's writing desk.

'Please, take it to the police as proof that Mr Hyde has left,' said Dr Jekyll. 'I hope he means what he says and that I can finally be free of him.' He gave a long, shuddering sigh and pulled his blanket further over his knees. 'Forgive me, Utterson, but I think I must rest now. I will see you very soon, I promise.'

Gabriel left Dr Jekyll feeling somehow more uneasy and more confused than when he had arrived. As Poole fetched his coat and hat, he asked: 'Poole, Dr Jekyll said that Mr Hyde delivered this letter this morning. Did Mr Hyde say where he was going when he left? Or did you perhaps see which direction he went in?'

Poole shook his head. 'I'm sorry, sir,' he began. 'But the only person who has called at the house today is you.'

Chapter Six

Gabriel stared at the letter Dr Jekyll had given him. It lay on his desk in his study and Gabriel could barely stand to touch it.

After thinking everything over, Gabriel had come to a conclusion. One of the following things must be true:

One: The letter really was from Mr Hyde, telling Dr Jekyll that he had run away and would never return. It had been delivered to

Dr Jekyll's house, but somehow Poole, the butler, had not seen it – or Mr Hyde.

Or two: Dr Jekyll was lying to protect Mr Hyde.

Gabriel hoped that the first answer was true. He hated to think that his friend would lie to him to cover the tracks of such a terrible man.

At that moment, Mr Guest came into the study with a tea tray. As he set it down on the desk, he said, 'Is that a letter from Dr Jekyll, sir?'

Gabriel looked from the open

letter to his secretary. 'Why do you ask that?'

'Why, sir, the writing is the same,' said Mr Guest, as if the answer was obvious.

Gabriel frowned and stood up. He went back to his tall cabinet and pulled out a document he had seen Dr Jekyll write with his own eyes. He laid the latest sheet of paper on the desk alongside the first.

'They look like completely different handwriting to me,' he said.

'Not *completely* different, sir,' Mr Guest corrected him. 'It is only that one slants forwards and the other

backwards.
Other than that,
they are identical.'

Gabriel looked again at the loops and swirls. 'My God, you're right!' he said.

The writing was the same. That meant that Dr Jekyll had faked the letter from Mr Hyde. He really was covering up for a murderer. But why? And what would happen to Dr Jekyll if Mr Hyde returned?

Chapter Seven

The sounds of music and laughter spilt from Dr Jekyll's house. Gabriel stood on the pavement outside, still unsure whether he should go in or not.

It had been two months since Sir Danvers Carew was cruelly killed, and there was still no sign of Mr Hyde. But last week, Gabriel had received an invitation to a party at Dr Jekyll's house.

'Hello, Utterson,' said a voice

behind him. It was Dr Lanyon.

'You were invited too, I see.'

Gabriel was a little shocked to see Dr Lanyon. The last time they had spoken about Dr Jekyll, he and Dr Lanyon were not on friendly terms.

'I was,' Gabriel replied. 'Although the last time I saw Dr Jekyll, he seemed quite unwell. I am surprised he has recovered enough to entertain again. Especially after all that horrible business.'

'With that Hyde fellow, you mean?' Dr Lanyon asked.

Gabriel nodded.

'Well,' the doctor sighed, 'we won't get any answers just standing out here. Let's go in and see what it is all about.'

Inside Dr Jekyll's house, the rooms were filled with people chatting and eating. Gabriel soon spotted Poole handing out food

to the guests from a silver tray.

'Mr Utterson, it is wonderful to see you,' he said, cheerfully handing Gabriel a drink.

'Thank you, Poole,' replied Gabriel. 'I can only assume your master is doing much better?'

Poole smiled. 'He is, sir,' he said. Then he lowered his voice.

'And we have not seen or heard anything from the dreadful Mr Hyde since that awful day. The doctor is much healthier and happier. He decided to throw a party to see all his *true* friends again, and show them that he is much recovered.'

Poole carried on handing out food while Gabriel searched for Dr Jekyll among the crowd. He soon spotted him having a lively conversation with Dr Lanyon. As their eyes met, Dr Jekyll beckoned Gabriel towards him.

'Utterson!' Dr Jekyll began. 'I am so grateful you decided to come – I was not sure if you would. The last time we spoke was under strange circumstances.'

'It was,' replied Gabriel, staring at Dr Jekyll's face. He looked much better. His eyes were brighter, and his skin was rosy. He was dressed smartly, and he no longer had that strange lost look in his eyes. 'I am glad to see you looking so well, Jekyll.'

'Thank you, my friend,' the doctor said. 'I am hoping to put all of that business in the past and move on – speaking of which, I must go and greet some more of my guests! Enjoy the party!'

For the rest of the evening, Gabriel spent his time talking to friends and enjoying the delicious food Dr Jekyll had put out. It was nearly midnight when Gabriel decided it was time to go. He looked for Dr Jekyll to thank him for a lovely evening and spotted him huddled in a corner once again with Dr Lanyon.

'Ah, Utterson are you leaving?' Dr Jekyll asked.

'I am. Thank you for a wonderful time,' Gabriel replied. 'Dr Lanyon, would you like to share a carriage home?'

Dr Lanyon looked between Gabriel and Dr Jekyll. 'Thank you, my boy, that is very kind, but Dr Jekyll wants to show me something before I go.'

Gabriel noticed that a serious look had fallen across Dr Lanyon's face. 'Are you sure?' he asked.

'He's quite sure!' answered Dr Jekyll, brightly. 'Safe journey home, Utterson!' And with that, the pair disappeared towards Dr Jekyll's courtyard.

Chapter Eight

As the weeks passed, Gabriel worried less and less about Dr Jekyll. He had been pleased to see his friend looking so well at the party, and he hoped that Mr Hyde would never again show his face. But if he did, he would be arrested for the murder of Sir Danvers Carew.

One evening, Gabriel found himself walking near to Dr Lanyon's house and decided to pay him a visit. He had not seen him since the night of Dr Jekyll's party.

Dr Lanyon's butler invited Gabriel inside, but warned him that his master had not been feeling very well these past few weeks.

'Oh, Utterson, I am so glad you have called,' said Dr Lanyon. Gabriel could immediately see that the doctor was indeed unwell. In fact, he reminded Gabriel of Dr Jekyll when *he* had been feeling unwell.

'I have wanted to pay a call on you myself, but as you can see, I have not been up to leaving the house.'

Gabriel sat next to Dr Lanyon on his comfortable sofa. 'What is wrong, my friend?' he asked.

Dr Lanyon stared into the fire. 'My heart is heavy and I feel weak all over,' he replied. 'I have treated so many people in my life, and now I can't seem to make *myself* feel better.'

'But what has caused you to feel this way?'

Dr Lanyon turned and stared

at Gabriel with familiar haunted eyes. He took Gabriel's hand.
'I have seen something terrible – something that is not of this world!'

Gabriel patted his friend's arm. 'Come now, "not of this world"? It is not like you to talk of such things!'

'Nevertheless, I fear I will never recover from the shock.'

'It cannot be as bad as all that,' Gabriel tried to reassure him. 'What can I do to help?'

Dr Lanyon pointed to a small side table with a sealed envelope on top. 'Take that envelope and keep it safe. I want you to open it, but only after I have died.'

Gabriel was shocked to hear the doctor talk of death. 'Oh, I am sure that won't be for a very long time!' he said, as cheerfully as he could.

'Please,' said Dr Lanyon again. 'I am trusting you to do this for me.'

Gabriel had no choice but to agree to the doctor's request.

***

After saying goodbye to Dr Lanyon, Gabriel tucked the envelope into his inside pocket. He could not shake the feeling that Dr Lanyon's illness and the letter all had something to do with Dr Jekyll and the night of the party.

He set off for Dr Jekyll's home, determined to find out more.

'Dr Jekyll is not seeing anyone at the moment, sir,' said Poole when Gabriel knocked on Dr Jekyll's door. 'He has been working very hard on his experiments these past few weeks and …'

'And what, Poole?' Gabriel asked, gently, sensing the butler's unease. He looked far more concerned than he had on the night of the party.

'And I am worried he is slipping back into his old ways,' Poole whispered.

'Has Mr Hyde returned?' Gabriel asked.

The butler shook his head. 'We have not seen him, sir,' he said. 'I shall let the doctor know you have called. I am sure he will want to see all his old friends again. Soon.'

Chapter Nine

Only a few weeks later, Gabriel received the sad news that his friend Dr Lanyon had died from his mysterious illness. Feeling miserable, he dressed in his black suit and top hat to attend the funeral.

Gabriel was glad to see so many of Dr Lanyon's friends and relatives at the funeral, ready to say goodbye to the kindly doctor. However, there was one face that was missing: Dr Jekyll's. This struck Gabriel as strange, since the two men seemed to have put their differences behind each other at Dr Jekyll's party and become friends again.

On returning to his study after the funeral, Gabriel took out the envelope Dr Lanyon had given him to open after his death. However, when Gabriel opened the wax seal, he saw that rather than a letter inside, there was another envelope. On this one were the words: *To be opened after the death of Dr Jekyll.*

Gabriel stared at the envelope in shock. Dr Jekyll was no longer in bad health, as far as he knew. And like himself and Dr Lanyon, he was only fifty.

What did it all mean?

Gabriel turned the new envelope over and over in his hands. He could open it there and then and get all the answers he needed, but that was not what Dr Lanyon had wanted, and he had to respect his friend's wishes. So, he placed the letter in his desk drawer, locked it and tried to concentrate on his work.

***

It was Sunday once again and Gabriel was pleased to be walking in the warm evening air with his

cousin, Richard. They talked about their families and the weather and a book they had both recently read. They were both so engrossed in their conversation that they did not realise they were approaching Dr Jekyll's laboratory door until they were there.

'Ah!' said Richard. 'Here we are again. At the spot where I saw that dreadful Mr Hyde knock down that poor girl. It was a long time ago

now, but I do still wonder about him – and this strange door.'

'It belongs to Dr Jekyll,' Gabriel revealed. 'You remember I mentioned that he is a friend and a client of mine? That is how I found out.'

'A doctor lives here?' Richard eyed the dingy building doubtfully.

'No, no,' said Gabriel. 'It is only his laboratory. The main house is behind it. I'll show you.' And he led his cousin around the corner and towards the parallel street where Dr Jekyll lived. As they walked, they continued talking.

'And what was the connection between Dr Jekyll and Mr Hyde?' asked Richard.

'Friends, at the time,' answered Gabriel, 'though not anymore.'

'I should think not!' said Richard. 'I believe Mr Hyde is now wanted for murder. Wait, is that him? Dr Jekyll, I mean.'

Gabriel had paused by the second house down from the left-hand corner. The middle of the three bottom windows was open and a man was sitting at a table inside it, looking as sad as a prisoner in a cell.

'Jekyll!' Gabriel called. 'Are you working on a Sunday? Why not take a break and join my cousin and I for a walk?'

'That would be love–' Dr Jekyll stopped halfway through his sentence as his eyes bulged and his face turned pink. 'I'm sorry …' he spluttered.

'Are you all right, Dr Jekyll?' called Richard, alarmed.

'Quite all right ...' said Dr Jekyll, although it was clear that he was not. He shut the window and pulled the curtains, leaving Gabriel and his cousin startled on the pavement.

Chapter Ten

Neither Gabriel nor his cousin could understand what had happened to Dr Jekyll to make him disappear from the window so suddenly. Back home in his study, Gabriel unlocked his desk drawer and once again looked at Dr Lanyon's envelope. He wondered if there was something inside that could help his friend, but before he had the chance to make a decision about opening it, there was a knock on his front door.

Poole was standing outside, looking more worried than Gabriel had ever seen him. 'I am terribly sorry to disturb you, sir,' he said, wringing his hands together. 'But I did not know who else to turn to.'

'What on earth is the matter, Poole?' asked Gabriel.

'It's Dr Jekyll, sir, please can you come at once?' asked Poole.

Gabriel grabbed his coat and hat and followed the butler who was already halfway down the street, rushing back to Dr Jekyll's home. The weather outside was wild and windy, but when they arrived, they found Dr Jekyll's servants gathered in the courtyard, ignoring the thin trees lashing the railings. They were talking in low voices, their arms around each other as they faced the laboratory at the opposite end of the cobblestones.

'He won't come out,' said the housekeeper.

'*He* won't *let* him out!' said one of the maids, in tears.

'Who?' asked Gabriel, making his way through the small crowd to Dr Jekyll's laboratory door. 'Poole, please tell me what is going on.'

Poole took a deep breath. 'After the party, Dr Jekyll started to spend more and more time in his laboratory. I have not seen him at all this past week. He keeps the door locked and shouts his orders through it when we knock.'

'Shouts? That does not sound like him at all,' said Gabriel.

'It's not!' said the housekeeper, who had also begun to cry. 'The doctor is always polite, but this week he has been horrible to all of us. Sometimes his voice sounds strange – different.'

Gabriel's frowned. 'Are you sure that the voice is Dr Jekyll's?' he asked. 'Perhaps Mr Hyde has returned and it is he who has been shouting orders through the door.'

'That's what I said!' said the tearful maid.

Poole nodded. 'That thought did

occur to us, sir,' he said, sadly. 'But I cannot always tell for sure. All he keeps asking for is salt.'

'Salt?'

'Yes, a special kind of salt imported from another country – we had it many months ago but have run out. Now, nowhere in London sells it and it is filling the doctor with rage.'

'If he even *is* the doctor,' the maid reminded the butler.

'Well,' sighed Gabriel. 'There's only one way to find out …'

Chapter Eleven

While Poole and the rest of the servants watched, Gabriel approached the door to the laboratory. He tried the handle. It was locked like Poole had said.

Gabriel could not understand what had happened to his friend to make him act so strangely, or to keep him locked away in his own laboratory. Could Mr Hyde be keeping him prisoner? And why did he need a special kind of salt so badly? There were too many questions and Gabriel was determined, finally, to get some answers.

'Jekyll!' he called. 'Jekyll, it's me, Utterson. Won't you let me in?'

'Go away!' came the reply, in a strange, strangled voice.

'We want to help you. Please, unlock the door,' Gabriel called.

'No one can help me now,' came the voice. 'It is all over!'

Gabriel turned to the butler. 'Poole, with your agreement, I think we should break down the door,' he said. Poole looked shocked and a little scared, but he nodded.

Gabriel raised his voice and spoke through the door again, 'Jekyll, we are coming in. On the count of three, we will break down this door.' All he heard in reply was the sound of breaking glass and furniture being knocked over. 'One!' Gabriel called, as Poole came to stand by him. 'Two!' he called, as he and Poole braced themselves, ready to push. 'Three!' With that, the two men set their weight against the door, broke the lock and went through.

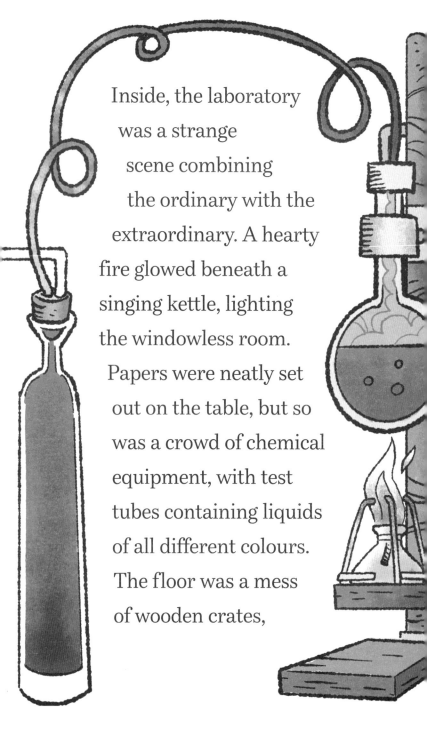

Inside, the laboratory was a strange scene combining the ordinary with the extraordinary. A hearty fire glowed beneath a singing kettle, lighting the windowless room. Papers were neatly set out on the table, but so was a crowd of chemical equipment, with test tubes containing liquids of all different colours. The floor was a mess of wooden crates, packing straw and freshly broken glass. In the middle of it all, beside a fallen stool, was the small, withered body of Mr Hyde. He lay perfectly still on the ground. He was wearing Dr Jekyll's clothes and shoes, which were all far too big for him. In his hands was a small bottle of blue liquid. As Gabriel came closer, he could see from the label that the bottle contained poison. It was open and empty.

Poole hurried the servants away, not wanting them to see the horrible sight. Gabriel searched the room and upstairs, but there was no sign of Dr Jekyll.

'But how can that be?' said Poole. 'I know he was in here. I heard him, I'm sure of it.'

'Call the police,' Gabriel told him.

After Poole left to follow his instruction, Gabriel spotted two envelopes on the table. They were addressed to him. Inside the first was a new will and a note asking Gabriel to read the letter he had been given by Dr Lanyon, then to read the letter in the second envelope.

Gabriel stared at the note and the will in confusion, until the sound of the police arriving shook him to his senses. He quickly put the papers inside his coat and prepared for more questions he would not be able to answer. Including where was Dr Jekyll?

Chapter Twelve

By the time Gabriel returned home, it was very late. Mr Guest had kindly waited up for him and kept the fire going in his study. He could see Gabriel was in shock and made him some soothing tea before leaving him alone for the night.

Gabriel took out the envelope from Dr Lanyon and placed it on his lap. He then reached inside his coat for the envelope from Dr Jekyll. He was tired and his head ached, but he needed to understand what had been happening these past few months more than he needed to sleep.

As far as he knew, Dr Jekyll was missing and not dead. Nevertheless, slowly, he opened Dr Lanyon's letter.

My dear Utterson,
If you are reading this letter, it means that both myself and Jekyll have passed away.

You may remember that I told you Jekyll and I had fallen out because of some experiments he was performing. In short, Jekyll believed that he could make a medicine that would separate a person's goodness from their badness. I believe he wanted to find a way to make mankind truly good; to stop our wicked urges from surfacing. He did not succeed – quite the opposite.

When you left Jekyll's party that night, Jekyll wished to show me something in his laboratory. It was the medicine he had been experimenting with: a collection of chemicals and a small pot of salt. As you know, I am a medical doctor, not a scientist like Jekyll, and I still did not approve. In the spirit of restoring our friendship, however, I listened. Jekyll asked me to take the chemicals and salt home and wait for someone to visit me at midnight the following evening. I confess, I thought he was pulling a trick on me, but I did as he asked.

The following evening, I waited up until midnight, and someone did indeed call. It was

Mr Hyde. I was appalled by his strange, hunched figure and rude way of speaking. I wanted to call the police straight away, but he pushed past me and headed straight to my study – he knew exactly where he was going, as though he had been to my house many times before. When he found the chemicals, he started mixing them together. Finally, he added the salt. The mixture bubbled and fizzed. Then Mr Hyde drank it!

What happened next, I must tell you, is the strangest and

most shocking thing I have ever witnessed. It is taking all the strength I have to simply write it down. When Mr Hyde had finished every last drop of the mixture, he began to stumble about. He fell to his knees and covered his face with his hands. Then, as he stood back up, the features on his face seemed to move about and he began to grow taller. Once he had settled, he faced me. Only he was not Mr Hyde any longer, but Jekyll. Mr Hyde had transformed into our old friend!

Jekyll explained that the medicine he had created did not stop a person's wicked urges from surfacing. Rather it transformed whoever took it into another person – the worst version of themselves, made up of all the bad and none of the good. It did not matter what Jekyll did as Mr Hyde, he could not feel sorry for it until he transformed back into himself.

I know this might sound like a fairy tale to you, Utterson, but I swear that every word is the truth. I have never had a strong heart, and seeing this strange and horrific sight weakened it even more. I cannot leave this world knowing that I did not tell anyone about what I saw. But I also did not want to be the cause of our misguided friend Jekyll going to prison.

You see, if Mr Hyde is caught and charged with the murder of Sir Danvers Carew, that means that Jekyll will be too. They are one and the same person. That is why I had to ask you to wait until

Jekyll's death (and therefore Mr Hyde's) for you to open this letter.

And now, I am at peace. I hope one day that you will be too, having put this terrible tale behind you.

Chapter Thirteen

Gabriel carefully folded Dr Lanyon's letter and placed it, with trembling hands, back in the envelope. Part of him wished he had never opened it. If only he could turn back the clock to a time when he would have laughed off such

a story as nonsense, instead of believing it as he did now.

Dr Jekyll and Mr Hyde were the same person. That is why Dr Jekyll had covered for and protected Mr Hyde.

The only thing Gabriel still did not know was why all this had happened in the first place. Dr Jekyll was a good man – not an angel, it was true, but a good man all the same. He was as likely to kill poor old Sir Danvers Carew as Gabriel was.

Gabriel suspected that the final answers lay in the second envelope. The envelope from Dr Jekyll.

> Utterson,
>
> Firstly, I want to thank you for opening and reading this letter. If you have already read dear Lanyon's letter, then you will know what I have become, and I would not have blamed you if you had thrown this letter into the fire unopened.

Let me start by explaining my life to you. When I was young, I inherited a lot of money. I did not have to work, but I was clever and healthy, and I wanted to study science. I went to university, as you know, and set up my own house with my own laboratory to conduct research.

There was another side to my personality that you may also remember. A darker side that enjoyed taking risks. I knew this side of me would one day get me into trouble, so I started trying to understand it through my research.

Please believe me, I did not set out to create the worst version of myself; I set out to create the best. I wanted to be better, Utterson. But once I became Hyde, once I knew what it was to do terrible things and not feel sorry for them ... Oh the freedom, Utterson!

It took years of work, and cost me my friendship with Lanyon, but finally I stumbled upon the mixture of chemicals that would create Hyde. And all I needed to do to return to myself as Jekyll was add a special kind of salt to the same mixture.

At first, as I said, I enjoyed turning into Hyde. He could do and say anything Jekyll wanted to but couldn't, and it satisfied that part of me that enjoyed making trouble without ruining my reputation. Once I'd had enough, I would take the second potion and change back into myself.

I found that I wanted to change into Hyde more and more. I even rented a flat for him and changed my will so that if I decided to stay as Hyde forever, he could use my house and money.

But then Hyde began to grow

stronger. And as he grew stronger, I began to grow weaker. You saw it yourself when you came to visit me and I was too weak to stand and greet you.

I knew it had gone too far when Sir Danvers Carew was murdered. Although it was I who had killed him, it did not feel like me. Hyde had completely taken over my body and I was powerless to stop him. I vowed from that day on that I would never change into Hyde again.

Chapter Fourteen

Gabriel had to stop reading to collect his thoughts. He could not believe how much Dr Jekyll had been keeping from him all this time. But he could believe that his intentions had been good at first. "I wanted to be better, Utterson" – the line repeated in Gabriel's mind and made the whole strange case that much sadder.

He returned to the letter.

After almost two months without transforming into Hyde, I was starting to feel much better. I arranged a party to show my friends that I was well again. However, a few nights before it was to take place, I awoke to find that I was transforming into Hyde without taking the potion. I scrambled to take the potion that changed me back into myself, and it worked as usual, but I was scared. If Hyde could already make me transform into him, what if he could one day stop me transforming back into myself?

That is when I asked for Lanyon's help. I gave him everything to make the antidote and asked him to take it home with him. I knew the only way to get him to help me was to show him what happened to me when I took it – something he would only believe if he saw it with his own eyes.

I am sure he has given you an account of that night. I have never seen a man more distressed. He threw me out of his house and I did not see him again. When I heard of his death, I knew that

it was because of the shock
I had given him. I was now
responsible for two deaths.

I found that I had to take
more and more of the potion
to keep myself as Jekyll, while
Hyde was taking over more
every day. That evening when
I closed the window on you
and your cousin, it was because
I felt the transformation
coming on. Then, I realised
that I was running out of
salt for the potion. No matter
how many different shops my
housekeeper visited, she could

not find the correct type.

I know now that Mr Hyde will soon take over completely, and I cannot let that happen. I have a bottle of poison that I keep for the moment when I know it is all over.

I am sorry if you have to play any part in the death of Mr Hyde, but know that I, Dr Jekyll, am a good man in my heart.

Gabriel closed the letter and put it next to Dr Lanyon's. His eyes filled with tears. He was angry at Dr Jekyll, but mostly he was saddened by the loss of his friends.

After a while, Gabriel took a deep breath, picked up the letters and tossed them into the fire. He watched until every last piece had turned to ash.

Epilogue

The police were glad to have found Mr Hyde at last and to close the case of Sir Danvers Carew's murder. Everyone presumed that Mr Hyde had also killed Dr Jekyll, who was never found. In a way, this was true, although it was only Gabriel who knew it.

The new will that Dr Jekyll had written stated that he wanted his house and all his possessions to go to Gabriel. It was a clever thing to do. It meant that Gabriel could go through Dr Jekyll's laboratory and destroy all his notes and any remaining chemicals. No one would know what Dr Jekyll had done and, more importantly, no one would be able to do the same thing again.

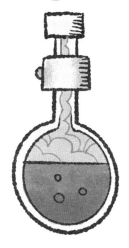

It was a cold Sunday evening many months later when Gabriel and his cousin set out once again for their weekly walk around the park.

'What a time you have had, cousin,' said Richard. 'Although I am glad that we no longer have to worry about Mr Hyde roaming the streets.'

Gabriel nodded in agreement and stared across the park at the setting sun.

'Do you think we will ever know what happened to your friend, Dr Jekyll?' Richard asked.

'I do not think so,' replied Gabriel. 'But I hope that like Lanyon, he is finally at peace.'

AUTHOR  BIOGRAPHY
Robert Louis Stevenson

Robert Louis Stevenson was born in Edinburgh in 1850. Despite very poor health, he wrote many books and travelled widely. His travels inspired him to write famous tales like *Treasure Island*, but the idea for *The Strange Case of Dr Jekyll and Mr Hyde* came to Stevenson in a fever dream when was he was ill. Today he is one of the most translated authors in the world.